A Perfect Pony

Gajitos

CHARMING PONIES

A Perfect Pony

LOIS SZYMANSKI

HarperFestival®
A Division of HarperCollins Publishers

HarperCollins®, ☕®, and HarperFestival®
are trademarks of HarperCollins Publishers Inc.

A Perfect Pony

All rights reserved. No part of this book may be used or reproduced
in any manner whatsoever without written permission except in the
case of brief quotations embodied in critical articles and reviews.
Printed in the United States of America. For information address
HarperCollins Children's Books, a division of HarperCollins
Publishers, 1350 Avenue of the Americas, New York, NY 10019.

www.harperchildrens.com

Library of Congress catalog card number: 96-96036

Typography by Sasha Illingworth

❖

First HarperFestival edition, 2005

For my wonderful daughter, Shannon
Szymanski. The patience and love you give
to your headstrong "princess" mare,
Christa, inspires and impresses me daily.

A Perfect Pony

one

Niki Crawford jumped out of the pickup truck almost before it had even stopped. Horses and riders milled about on the edge of the parking lot, and a long, blue horse trailer was backing up to a ramp that led into the stockyard. Floodlights lit the whole area, including the white letters on the side of the building that read LIVESTOCK AUCTION.

"Wait up, Niki!" Dad puffed as he slid out of the driver's seat. "Those horses aren't going anywhere without you."

Niki turned and grinned at her dad, her dark eyes twinkling. He was older than most of her friends' fathers, but the thinning gray hair and the slight limp didn't bother Niki. He was still "good ol' Dad." They had been on their own for as long as Niki could remember. Her mother had died when Niki was young.

Slowing her step, she waited for her father. She felt for the lump of rolled money in her back pocket, running her hand over it to make sure it was still there. A ripple of nervous jitters ran through her. *Tonight's the night*, she thought. *I'm finally going to get my own horse.*

Dad put a hand on Niki's long dark hair, and they walked inside together. "Nervous?" he asked, and she nodded.

"I can't believe it's finally happening," she said out loud.

"You earned it," Dad answered matter-of-factly. "That was the deal. You earn it. You pay for it. You take care of it." He paused. "The hard part's ahead of you."

Niki frowned as she looked into her Dad's blue eyes. "You know I'll take care of it. I've wanted a horse for so long . . ." her voice trailed off; then she added softly, "I can't wait to take care of it."

Inside the auction barn Dad stopped to talk to old friends, and Niki wandered down the aisles. They had come here every Saturday night since Niki was little. Dad came to visit with friends from neighboring farms. Niki came for the horses.

Inside the ring, she heard the auctioneer beginning to sell the tack. She knew they would sell the saddles and bridles, brushes and tools for at least another hour before the horses and ponies were led in.

As Niki came to the first row of horses, she stopped to evaluate each one. She was looking for the perfect pony, the pony of her dreams. Would it be a chestnut or a bay, a pinto or a gray? It didn't matter to Niki what color it was. What mattered was something else. Maybe a certain look in its eye or the way it carried itself. Heck, she wasn't even quite sure what it would be. But she was sure that she would know it when she saw her special horse. She would just know.

In the first square pen was a tall, chestnut thoroughbred with two white stockings. He paced from side to side and threw back his head, his eyes rolling wildly. Sticking her head through the top two rails, Niki peered up at the chestnut. All at once he drew himself up and let out a loud whinny. Niki jumped so quick that she bumped her head on the top rail.

She rubbed her head as she moved on to the next pen. There she looked in at a tiny pinto mare with a young foal at its side. A crowd was already gathering around this pen, and Niki knew that the pair would bring a high price. She called it the "cute factor." Whenever there was a fuzzy or cute or young pony, the crowd would "ooh" and "ahh" and the animals would sell for a high price. She moved on.

Down the row she looked at a sturdy bay pony saddled in Western gear. He looked like a nice pony, but not special. She studied a dapple gray yearling for quite some time. It seemed sensitive enough, but it would be another year until she could ride it. There were two pintos—a tall, rangy looking sorrel and a stocky blood bay. Nothing special. Niki was beginning to get discouraged.

She'd worked so hard this summer, helping on the farm, earning the money the hard way, like Daddy said she had to, and now . . . where was her pony?

Turning back to the blue trailer, Niki watched as the driver and his partner returned from the business office to unload their cargo. The first one off was a magnificent black-and-white pinto with a flowing black tail. Niki felt her heart pound as she watched it come down the aisle, right past her and into a holding pen. But if she was impressed with the pinto, she was totally unprepared for the next one.

Her breath caught in her throat as she watched a pure white mare come off the trailer and down the ramp. The mane hung in long silvery strands and she held her head high. She was calm, Niki noticed. That was a trait she was looking for. But there was even more. A large pony, the mare was just the right height. She picked her hooves up daintily as she stepped through the dirty stockyard, almost as if it was not quite clean enough for her.

"Princess," Niki mumbled. The pony was an absolute princess. Then it came down the aisle right beside her, and Niki felt her heart explode as the mare tossed her head. By the time they had closed the gate of the holding pen, Niki was really excited. She reached back to feel the money in her pocket and she knew it would be enough. "Princess" was the one.

When the men had penned her and the vet had finished drawing blood from her neck for the required health check, Niki sidled closer. The man who had led the mare down the ramp and into the pen was a cowboy with a wide-brimmed hat. Now, as he left the pen, he slapped a sticker on the mare's rump: 56. Princess was number 56. It etched itself into

Niki's brain. The number she needed to bid on would be 56. The cowboy grinned at her. "She's a good one, little miss," he said, and Niki blushed. Was it so obvious that she was taken with the mare?

After the men had left, Niki clucked to the mare and she came right over. The face was long and dish-shaped, like an Arabian, with a tiny teacup nose and wide, deep-set eyes. They were soft and brown and they watched Niki closely as she reached through the rails to pat the horse on the shoulder. Without hesitation, the mare lowered her head and her velvety muzzle settled into Niki's hand. *With a spiraled horn she could be a unicorn from a fairy tale*, Niki thought.

There was a commotion behind her and a high-pitched whine rang out. "I want that one, Mamma! You gotta git me that one over there!"

A heavyset woman with rosy cheeks and a big stain on the front of her too tight T-shirt was coming down the aisle. With her hand clasped firmly in his, she was fairly dragging along a chubby little boy with a crew cut. But the whine had not come from the small child. It had come from nine-year-old Billy Baily. Niki knew him. He was in her class at school and he was a royal pain. Now he was pointing at her Princess.

Then he caught sight of Niki. "Hey! It's N*iiii*ki!" he crooned. "Icky, picky, sticky, Niki! Whatta you doin' here, Icky?"

Niki whirled around with her hands on her hips. "Same thing as you, Billy," she said. "It's a free country."

Instead of answering her Billy stuck his fingers in his ears and twirled them around, his tongue hanging out the side of his mouth and his eyes rolling up.

Niki turned and marched down the aisle, away from Billy and away from Princess. "Some people never grow up . . . Billy!" she said over her shoulder.

As Billy's whiney voice faded behind her, Niki hurried forward. There was a crowd gathered around another holding pen where a pony had just been unloaded. *Probably another "cute factor,"* she thought, but she knew she had to see for herself.

She heard the comment of a lady in front of her before she even saw the pony. "Poor, dear thing," the lady said under her breath.

After pushing her way through the sea of legs and bodies gathered around the rails, Niki knelt down and peered into the pen through the bottom rails. The pony was a little bit shorter than Princess, coal black with four white stockings and a narrow white blaze running down the length of his face. She could see his face clearly because it was hanging down to his knees, which were buckled from the sheer energy of holding himself up. Every rib protruded in agonizing detail and he heaved soft whuffing breaths. If it weren't for the way his spindley legs were braced, he would surely have been on the ground.

Niki's heart, which moments ago had danced with happiness, now dropped to her stomach. She fought a sick feeling that was oozing up from inside of her as she looked into the pony's glazed eyes.

"The doggers will buy this one for sure," she heard someone say and others grunted in agreement.

❀ 9 ❀

No! she thought angrily. How could they say that? How could they let the dog food buyers get him before he even had a chance? He had already suffered enough. Then, to die for that . . . to become canned dog food! It just wasn't fair.

Niki's hand snaked through the rails to stroke the pony's long white blaze. Slowly, the pony lifted his black head and met her gaze. He held her stare for a moment before dropping his head back down again. But that moment was all it took.

two

Niki wiggled in her seat and watched as the thoroughbred was led out of the ring, prancing and dancing like a ballerina on his back hooves. She reached into the tub of popcorn that was braced between her knees. Popping a handful into her mouth, she waited for her dad to come back with sodas.

Next, a little girl with two long braids rode in on

the bay pony that wore the Western saddle. Dad settled in the seat beside Niki and handed her a soda. "So, you gonna bid on the white mare?" he asked.

Niki stared ahead at the little girl circling the ring on the pony. Niki had showed her dad the mare, and she thought that was her choice, but she couldn't shake the picture of the broken-down pony from her mind. "Can I buy two if I have enough money?" she asked.

Dad twittled his thumbs and shook his head. "What in tarnation would you do with two ponies?"

"I could take care of two."

"Not until you prove you can take care of one. One pony, Niki. That was the deal."

"But, Dad . . ."

"No buts, missy. How many girls get a pony of their own? Now, it will be your pony and you can bid on any one here, but one is your limit."

Niki watched as the bay pony was led out of the ring. It had gone for two hundred dollars, a good price for a nice little pony. Niki knew the white mare would go for more, but that was okay. She had five hundred fifty dollars. *Think with your head*, she told herself, *not with your heart*. The white one, she decided. I have to have the white one. *What would I do with a broken-down pony, anyway?*

Niki munched her popcorn slowly as the horses came and went from the ring. She listened to the hum of the auctioneer's voice as he shouted numbers and acknowledged bids.

As she sipped her soda, two men led the black pony in. They walked slowly, supporting the shaky body on both sides. With his head down, he looked up at the crowd and sighed loudly. His ribs were heaving with every breath he took, and Niki's heart sank again as she watched him.

The bidding started at a measly ten dollars and went up by fives instead of fifties. A family in the front row put in a pity bid, but a loud counterbid came from heavyset Brandon Bartell, the meat man!

"Twenty dollars!" the man with the family in the front row called out.

"Geez," Niki said with disgust.

"Twenty-seven," Bartell countered calmly.

"He's yours," the man in the front said. "He's not worth it."

"Okay," the auctioneer hummed. "We've got a twenty-seven-dollar bid on the black pony. Going once. Going twice."

Niki stood up and shouted. "Fifty dollars!"

As if in slow motion, the popcorn tumbled from between her legs, spraying down the row of empty seats in front of her, and at the same time every head in the auction barn turned to stare.

There was dead silence for at least thirty seconds. Niki felt herself blush, but she also felt anger mounting. *How dare they treat this pony like—like—well, like dog meat. He's a living, breathing pony, for crying out loud, and he's worth more than twenty-seven dollars!*

The auctioneer had composed himself during those few seconds, and now he continued. "We've got a bid of fifty dollars, Mr. Bartell. Would you like to up that bid?"

"Heck no. He's not worth that. Not even for meat."

Niki steamed inside.

"Going once. Going twice. Sold to the girl in the back there. What's your number, honey?"

Niki rooted in her back pocket and pulled out the cardboard stub with her number written on it. She held it up for him to see.

"Eighty-one," the auctioneer said, and the secretary recorded it in her book. Niki stood up and started to leave, a mix of emotions stirring inside of her. She'd saved the pony from becoming dog food, but at what cost? This was not the pony of her dreams. He wasn't even close.

Before she'd even stepped around her dad, she heard the audience gasp. She turned and saw the princess. The perfect pony was strutting into the ring, her head held proud, her manners impeccable. Niki felt a wrench of anger and pain inside of her and she sank into her seat again.

She watched the perfect pony circle the ring

quietly and a moan formed on her lips. She still had five hundred dollars left of her original five hundred fifty. She turned to her father. "Dad? Can I bid on her, too?"

Dad's eyes filled with compassion, and for a moment she hoped he'd change his mind, but then he shook his head slowly. "You made your choice, honey. I'm sorry, but one is all we can handle."

Niki turned numbly to watch the bidding begin. It went quickly, starting at one hundred dollars. Niki groaned again when she realized that the mare had sold for five hundred fifty dollars, exactly what she had saved. She stood and picked her way out of the seat, heading down to the holding pens. She had to see the black pony. After all, he was hers.

The pony was alone. No crowd gathered around his pen this time. They were all inside, *bidding on the magnificent horses*, Niki thought ruefully. She opened the gate and slipped inside. Her father had stayed in his seat. Maybe he realized that she needed to be alone with her feelings.

The pony was standing in the far corner of the pen. He looked at Niki warily as she entered, but made no attempt to move.

"Hi, little boy," she said softly, stepping nearer as she spoke. The pony raised his head and watched her closely, mistrust in his eyes. "You don't have to worry about a thing anymore," Niki continued. "I'm going to take good care of you."

The pony sighed loudly and lowered his head. Niki slid a hand down his neck, then held his head under the jaw and lifted it gently. The pony looked into her eyes and Niki thought she saw hope. No. It was her imagination. But it did feel good to know that she had single-handedly saved the black pony from certain death. She rubbed his head softly, down the white blaze, running her fingers over the whiskery muzzle.

"Hey, Icky!" Billy's shrill voice rang out. "Bought a real nag, didn't you?"

Niki refused to turn around, refused to look at Billy Baily.

"Too bad you didn't buy a nice horse like me. Look at my perfect horse!"

Niki fought down the anger. She turned slowly, hopelessness settling over her. She knew before she even looked which horse Billy Baily had bought.

The princess looked haughtily down at the chubby boy who held her lead. She picked her way down the aisle and back into her holding pen, her neck arched with dignity.

Billy Baily had bought the princess. *My princess*, Niki thought. *My perfect horse.*

three

Niki could not stand to watch Billy yank the beautiful mare around the stockyard, so she went back inside with her dad to watch the rest of the bidding. Only when Billy was gone did Niki return to the black pony. Then she combed his mane with her fingers and whispered softly to him. "You will get fat and shiny," she promised, "and no one will ever treat you bad again." *It was a good thing she had lots of money left*, Niki reasoned. She would need it for the vet bills, medications, and all the food it would take to fatten up the half-starved pony.

After the last horse had been sold, Dad helped Niki load her pony into the back of the pickup truck. He tied the lead shank to the sideboards and hung a bag of hay in front of the pony. Listlessly, the pony pulled out pieces of hay and munched them slowly.

On the way home, Dad placed his hand on Niki's knee. "You did a good thing," he said. "That pony needed you, and you were there for him. He'll fatten up. You'll see."

Niki fussed with her seatbelt. She wanted to feel good. She really did. But all she could see when she closed her eyes was Billy Baily pulling her princess around the stockyard.

"With all that love you have just bursting inside of you, you'll turn his life around. He'll be a good little pony when you're done with him," Dad reassured her. "He's got a lot of heart to have hung in

❀ *20* ❀

there for this long."

"You don't think he will die?"

"Heck, no. He's a young thing. He'll come back. You'll see."

"How old do you think he is?"

"I took a peek at his teeth at the auction barn and I don't think he's old at all. I'd say . . . maybe three or four. His molars aren't in yet."

"Three or four?" Niki was shocked. "I thought he was old."

"Mistreatment can make a pony age fast, and that poor thing has had the worst of it. But we're going to change all that, aren't we, Sunshine?"

Niki grinned at her dad. "Three or four," she mused out loud. "Do you think he's been trained to carry a rider yet?"

"I seriously doubt it. He looks like he's been ignored for a long time." Dad put his hand back on the wheel as he turned into their lane. "It makes me fighting mad when I see what folks can do to a pony," he said. "They go out and buy their kids a pony just

❀ 21 ❀

because it's cute and the kids want it. They don't have time to fool with it, so the pony gets tied in the backyard where it gets outgrown. Then it's neglected until it comes to this." He jerked his thumb back toward the black pony. "He needs to be wormed, washed, have his hooves trimmed, a good grooming . . ." Dad checked off a list of things the pony needed. Then he stopped and looked at Niki. "Anything else?" he asked.

"To be loved," Niki said simply. "He needs to be loved."

On Sunday morning Niki found the pony waiting patiently in the stall where they had left him the night before. He had eaten some of the hay they had left in the rack, and there was a place in the corner of the straw that was smashed down as if he had rested during the night. Niki smiled as she unlatched the door and went in to see her new pony. She carried a bucket with a hoof pick, a curry comb, a show brush, and an assortment of rags into the stall.

"Hi, handsome," she sang out, smiling at her choice of words. With his ribs jutting out and his knees nearly buckled, he was anything but handsome. *At least he seems stronger*, Niki thought. She ran a hand down his neck and was pleased to see that he stood steadily, unwavering on his feet. Just one night of rest, a handful of oats and a flake of hay had made him seem stronger.

She began to rub a rag down his neck and over his withers, gently scrubbing away some of the layers of mud and dirt. "We need a name for you," she told him as she worked. "I could call you Prince," she said, then just as quickly she erased the idea from her mind. He was not a substitute for the princess. "We need a name that is earthy and strong," she mused out loud, "like you."

As she talked, the pony turned his eyes to stare at her, then rubbed his head up and down against her arm, almost in affection. "You're a sweetie, aren't you?" Niki asked him. She pulled the show brush out of the bucket and finished working the dirt out of his neck. He was starting to shine in the spots that she had brushed, and inside she was beginning to shine, too. He was a nice pony, not drop-dead gorgeous, not stunningly elegant, but nice. Real nice.

"Blackie. Blaze. Ashes. Moonbeam." She tried the names on like clothing, tossing them aside just as quickly when she found they didn't fit. "What is your name?" she asked the pony. By now she was using the curry comb on his back, scrubbing in circular motions to remove the dirt and dust. As it rose to the surface, she used the softer show brush to sweep it away.

"Smokey, Cowboy, Berry . . ." She was singing the names out loud now as quickly as she thought of them. At the same time she moved the soft brush down his legs, stopping to pick clumps of mud off with her fingernail before brushing again.

"I like that last one."

Niki nearly jumped out of her skin at Dad's deep voice. "Geez, Dad! You scared me to death! I didn't hear you come up."

"Is my voice that scary?"

"No, I just didn't know you were there."

"Ummm," Dad smiled. "I did like that last name though. Barry. A good name for a boy."

"Daaad," Niki moaned. "I didn't mean that kind of Barry. I meant like strawberry, raspberry . . . blackberry."

All at once Niki stopped grooming and straightened up. "Blackberry!" she said again. "For a black pony . . . I like it!"

The pony turned a narrow white blaze to face Niki. Then he rubbed his head against her arm again and she grinned.

"You like that name too, don't you, boy? Then, Blackberry it is!"

As Dad carried the water bucket outside the stall to refill it for Niki, she hummed softly. Things were going to work out just fine after all!

Dad brought the fresh water in and sat it down in the corner of the stall. Niki put the brushes back in her bucket of grooming tools and pulled out a hoofpick, a metal tool that curved into a point on the end. As she lifted Blackberry's front leg to clean out his hoof, a terrible stench filled the air. Without stopping, she began to pick the v-shaped groove in the bottom of his hoof. But the odor just got worse, until she thought she could pass out from smelling it. Then she noticed that the hoof looked shadowy and it seemed to ooze, runny and gray.

"*Whoa*!" Dad said as the smell reached his nostrils.

Niki dropped the hoof and straightened up. "What's wrong with his hooves? They're soft and runny and . . . uh, disgusting!"

"I saw," Dad said. "It looks like your Blackberry has a bad case of thrush."

Niki felt her happiness begin to slowly seep away. She straightened up and pushed her head into Blackberry's warm neck for comfort. Thrush. It sounded bad. It smelled bad. It looked bad. And it was in the worst place: his hooves.

four

D r. Booth lifted Blackberry's hoof up until it rested on his bent leg. He checked the outer edge for cracking, then pulled the hoof down so that he could examine the underside. One at a time, he checked each hoof. As he examined the pony, once again the smell rose up, like mist sprayed from a perfume bottle, only it didn't smell anything like perfume.

Niki clasped a hand over her nose and mouth. She felt the tears behind her eyelids burn. Anything that smelled that horrible had to be bad news. *Please, God. Just don't let him be lame*, Niki begged silently. She knew that if a pony could not walk, it could not be saved.

Dr. Booth cleared his throat and put the hoof down. He pushed his wire-frame glasses back up and off his nose as he stood up. "Actually, it isn't that bad," he said.

Niki slid her hands down her face and over her chin and waited to hear more.

"It's thrush, all right. But it could have been a lot worse. You got this pony just in time." Dr. Booth reached into his black case and pulled out a tube. He handed it to Dad, then he turned to Niki. "Is he your pony?" he asked.

Niki nodded and Dr. Booth continued. "Listen carefully," he said, and Niki nodded again. "I'm going to trim his hooves before I go. Then, I want you to clean his hooves every morning and every night. After you clean them, you need to get a piece of cotton like this." He handed Niki a piece of white material. "Wrap the cotton around the hoof pick, soak it with the medicine, and reach deep into the crevices of his hoof. Take care to get lots of medicine into every part of his hoof."

Dr. Booth snapped his black case closed and straightened up.

"Is that all?" Niki asked.

Already Dr. Booth had lifted a front hoof and he was trimming away the deadened edges. He talked as he worked, moving from hoof to hoof with the big pair of clippers. "If you keep his stall clean and dry and use the medicine like I told you, this little guy should be as good as new in about three days."

"Three days!" Niki exclaimed in disbelief. "He will really be better in just three days?" The smell of those hooves made it seem impossible.

Dr. Booth slipped the clippers into his back pocket and gathered up his tools. "Yes," he answered.

Dad carried Dr. Booth's bag to his truck for him. "That poor little guy has a long way to go yet," Dad said, then his voice became proud, "but if anyone can nurse him back to health, it's my Niki."

Dr. Booth smiled and turned to Niki. "There is something else I should have told you," he added. "Exercise him daily. It will make his hooves heal quicker and it will help him gain his strength back, too."

"How did his hooves get that way?" Niki asked.

"Thrush comes from standing around in dirty stalls with manure up to the knees or even from muddy lots. Clean horses and ponies don't get thrush."

Niki grimaced. Already she was beginning to love Blackberry, and it made her angry to think of how horrible he had been treated. *How could anyone do that to my Blackberry?*

Dr. Booth had climbed in his truck and was ready to leave when Niki thought of something else. She ran back down the driveway just as he was about to pull away.

"How soon until you think I can ride him?" she asked.

"I think after a week of good food and nutrition he'll be ready to start." Dr. Booth sized up Niki. "You're a tiny thing," he mused. "You won't hurt him one bit." Then he drove out the lane, the gravel crackling under his tires like popcorn just beginning to pop.

Only a week, Niki thought. Throwing her arms up in the air, she began to spin and dance. The hooves would be better in three days and he would be ready to start riding in just a week. *My pony will get better and be a prince as perfect as the princess*, Niki thought. Then she danced down the lane and back to the barn where Blackberry was waiting.

five

On Monday, Billy Baily started to brag about his perfect horse as soon as he got on the bus. He had been in so much trouble during the year that he had been assigned a permanent seat in the front of the bus where Miss Sherry, the bus driver, could keep an eye on him.

"You should see my horse," Billy said. He turned around to face everyone. "She's tall and white and exceptionally beautiful," he boasted. He slid the word *exceptional* out over his tongue roughly, as if he was trying it out for the first time.

"Whoa," Niki whispered to her friend, Laura. "Billy knows a big word!" Laura grinned.

"Since she is so big and tough, I named her Warrior," Billy continued. "She's a real warrior!"

Geez, Niki thought. Warrior? It was the worst name he could have given to the princess.

Next, Billy rotated in his seat to face Niki. "Hey, Icky," he yelled, so that everyone on the bus could hear. "Tell us about the pony that you bought. Tell us about your bag of bones." Then he stood up. "She bought a real nag!" he yelled.

The girls on the bus giggled and the boys jeered. Niki slid down in her seat. *Billy is such a jerk*, she thought. *He doesn't deserve the princess.*

"Niki's pony can barely walk. He's falling apart at the seams!" Billy burst into a round of giggles at his own joke. Others on the bus joined in.

"Sit down, Billy," Miss Sherry said. Billy

wrinkled his nose at the bus driver's order, but he sat down.

"Ignore him," Laura whispered. "He just wants attention."

"I know." Niki sighed. "But my pony isn't a nag," she said. "He was just mistreated, and he's already getting better."

"Billy should understand that," Laura said.

"What do you mean?"

"Well, I hear that Billy's family isn't exactly nice. My mom said his dad is pretty mean to Billy."

Niki stared at Laura, taking in the shoulder-length brown hair and the soft brown eyes. "I didn't know," she said. *But that would explain a lot*, Niki thought to herself. Such as why Billy was so mean and why he always had to have attention, even if it got him into trouble. She just hoped he wasn't mean to the princess.

By Friday Niki was sick of hearing Billy Baily's picking and bragging. She was glad to have the week over.

After school she dropped her books inside and hurried to the barn to see Blackberry. He was in the small pasture, and he came running when he saw her approach. He let loose with a high-pitched whinny and pranced up to the gate. Already he looked better. The spaces between his ribs were filling in, and he was shiny from the grooming Niki gave him each day. His hooves had healed and they looked normal now.

He's actually pretty, Niki thought, and she beamed with pride! Niki slipped between the fence rails. Blackberry shoved his nose against her with a greeting that was so exuberant that it almost knocked her over. "Easy, boy," she said, but there was laughter in her voice.

She clipped a lead shank to his halter and tied him to the fence. After running a brush over his body to remove any dust or dirt, she leaned into his neck, breathing in the soft warm smell of horse. "Want to give me a ride?" she whispered.

Blackberry turned to look at her, his eyes wide and searching, like he wanted to understand. Niki rubbed his blaze gently. "We'll go slow," she told him. Then, Niki hurried to the barn to gather up the old saddle and bridle her dad had given her to ride with. They weren't fancy or new, but they had been her dad's when he was a boy, so to Niki the tack was special.

Soon Niki was slipping the saddle blanket and then the saddle onto Blackberry's back. She moved slowly so Blackberry could see what she was doing. The pony watched calmly as Niki tightened the cinch. *I bet he's been ridden before*, Niki thought to herself, then laughed when Blackberry nodded his head up and down as if he understood.

A moment later, Niki slipped the bridle onto her pony's head. She led Blackberry to the middle of the field. She leaned over his back and he stood quite still, so Niki slid a foot into the stirrup. In one quick, easy motion, Niki was in the saddle. She grasped the reins and waited for Blackberry to react. But Blackberry continued to stand. Slowly he turned his head around to look at Niki, and his look said, "*What are you doing on my back?*"

Niki burst into laughter—an uncontrolled, unbridled laughter. She had expected him to sidestep, or buck, or take off running. She had expected him to react in some way, but instead he just peered up at her with astonishment. As she laughed, he snorted and shook his head.

Niki squeezed his sides gently with her knees. "Come on boy," she said. "That's your signal to walk."

But Blackberry was staring at the nearby hedgerow, then he stopped and swiveled his head around to look at her again. "*Is that what you want?*" he seemed to be asking.

Niki slid from Blackberry's back and wrapped her arm under his neck, scratching his jaw. "You're something else," she said with a smile.

Suddenly Blackberry's head flew up and he stared at the hedgerow again. Niki stood still, this time hearing a crackling in the undergrowth. It sounded too loud to be a rabbit.

Niki walked closer. She bent down to peer into the bushes and leaves. There, in a gap in the brush, a figure was sitting crosslegged, watching Niki and Blackberry. He was muddy and alone and his face was stained with tears. The figure was Billy Baily.

six

"Billy Baily!" Niki exclaimed, her hands moving to her hips. "Are you spying on me?"

Billy crawled out of the bushes, rubbing the mud from his pants, then running a fist over his face. The effort only caused the mud to smear down his cheeks. "Naw," he said. "I was just watching you."

"It's the same thing," Niki said. "What are you doing here?"

"Where?"

"Here!" Niki pointed down angrily. "Here, on my farm!"

Billy scuffed at the ridges of dried mud in the pasture with an equally muddy work boot. "I was looking for my horse," he said so low that Niki could barely hear him.

"You were what?" Niki asked.

"Looking for my horse!" This time Billy nearly shouted. "She dumped me!" Billy glared at Niki. "Are you satisfied?

Niki felt the smile spread over her face as easy as butter on hot toast. She knew she shouldn't smile, but she couldn't help herself. "That's what you get for naming her Warrior," she snapped. Then she turned on her heel and began to stomp away, pulling Blackberry along beside her.

"Wait!" Billy called. "How did you get that pony to be so good?" he asked.

Niki stopped and turned. Billy didn't seem the same. He wasn't taunting. He wasn't teasing, and he wasn't picking. He wasn't being mean. He was serious.

"Billy." She sighed. "Why should I tell you? All you ever do is pick on me and embarrass me in front of my friends."

Billy looked like he was about to cry, and by the look of his face, Niki felt sure he had already been crying. She felt her mood soften. As much as she didn't want to, she was beginning to feel sorry for Billy. Instead of answering his question, she asked him one. "Why did Prin—I mean, Warrior, dump you?"

Billy shrugged. "I don't know." He reached over to stroke Blackberry. "I wanted her to run so I gave her a whack with the crop and she just bucked me off—as easy as that." He raised his palms up. "Then she ran away."

"You whacked her!" Niki could feel her blood begin to boil. That same old feeling of anger began to burn inside of her again. "You whacked a beautiful horse like that. She's a princess!" Niki exclaimed. "But you—you—" she stuttered with anger. "You are a *toad*."

Billy stared at Niki, wide-eyed but calm, as she exploded. "I am not a toad, Niki. Sometimes I act like one. But I am not a toad."

"Only a toad would whack a horse with a crop. If you aren't a toad, then why did you do a thing like that?"

"My dad told me to. He said that was how to make a horse go."

Niki rubbed Blackberry's neck. She didn't know what to say. If Billy's dad hit horses, would he hit Billy, too? Niki hoped not. Blackberry stretched his nose down and sniffed Billy's boots. Then a long tongue snaked out and he licked the toe of Billy's boot.

"Billy," Niki said. "You don't have to hit a horse to make it go. You asked me how I got Blackberry to go so good. Well, I'm going to tell you. It wasn't by hitting him. It was by loving him. My dad says if I love and respect Blackberry, he will love and respect me, and that will make him *want* to do what I ask."

Billy had moved closer to Niki now and he rubbed his dirty face again. His blond hair stuck up in spikes like an over-grown crewcut.

"You wouldn't respect someone who hit you, would you?" Niki asked.

Billy looked down as if in thought, and he scuffed his toe in the dirt again. Then slowly he shook his head. "No. I don't," he said simply. Niki felt the impact of the words hit her and at that moment she wished she liked Billy Baily, because she didn't want him to hurt anymore.

Impatient with standing so long, Blackberry began to paw the dirt with his front hoof. Niki reached over and unhooked the lead shank so that he could wander away, but he only went a few feet, then turned to watch them with a look of curiosity.

"How did you get him to look so good, so fast?" Billy asked. "No offense, Niki, but he was practically dead the night you bought him. Now, he shines."

"He just looked half dead," Niki answered. "My dad says mistreatment can make a horse age fast. Blackberry wasn't treated very well by whoever owned him before me. But he's treated well now," she added.

"You named him Blackberry," Billy said. "That's a good name. It fits him."

"Thanks," Niki said. She wanted to tell him that Warrior was a terrible name, but she didn't.

"Will you help me find Warrior?"

Niki didn't want to leave Blackberry, but it was starting to get dark and Billy looked like he would cry, so she nodded.

"Thanks, Niki." Billy squeaked. "You have a way with horses. And if I don't find Warrior, my dad will kill me."

Niki's eyes widened.

"Don't look like that, Niki," Billy said. "He won't *really* kill me, but I'll be in big trouble."

"Then let's get moving," Niki said. "Which way did she go?" And with that Niki followed Billy through the hole in the hedge and across the big back pasture.

seven

Billy led the way down an old dirt path, through a field of weeds and scattered briar bushes. Niki followed him silently for a while. As they walked, Niki scolded herself. After all the things Billy Baily had done to her, she couldn't believe she was out helping him find his horse.

"After Warrior dumped me she ran past your house, and then up that hill," Billy said. He pointed to the top of a grassy hill. It wasn't far at all. It was a hill that Niki could see from Blackberry's pasture. There was a small grove of trees at the top.

"Why didn't you go after her?"

Billy's shoulders slumped. "She wouldn't let me come near her. Every time I came close, she just danced away. Then she took off and up the hill. That's when I heard you talking to your pony. I was out of breath, so . . ."

Billy paused and rubbed his face. Niki wondered if that was when he had started to cry.

"So I stopped to rest and watch you," he said.

Billy was gazing right into Niki's eyes and it made her nervous. She looked away, picked up her step and started up the hill. The trees were shadowy, especially in the pre-dusk light, but she thought she saw something moving between the trunks and branches.

Billy was looking into the trees, too. "Do you think that's her?" he asked.

Niki shrugged, then broke into a jog. As she entered the grove of pines and whispering maple trees she felt the silence envelop them. She stood still. Breathing heavily from her run, she swiveled her head to look around, scanning the trees. A crunch of brush disrupted the stillness.

"It's her. There she is," Billy whispered loudly.

As quickly as Niki's eyes found the white princess, the princess had found them, too. Her ears were at attention. She had heard Billy's loud whisper and now intently she watched Niki and Billy.

Billy moved forward. His hand was outstretched and he whispered gentle-sounding words, but the princess was having none of it. She snorted and side-stepped as Billy tried to approach her, then danced away. Her head held high, she stayed just out of Billy's reach.

When he had had enough, Billy dropped his hand to his side and stomped over to Niki. "Do you see what I mean? Ohhhhh!" He swung his fist at a hanging branch. "How will I ever catch her?" he whined.

"Let me try," Niki offered.

She moved toward the mare quickly but quietly,

her palm outstretched, but curled up, as if a treat might just be inside for the mare's taking. At the same time she sang out a string of silly words. "You are such a princess pony. I wish you were my own. If I give you a carrot and promise you a bag, will you follow me back home? Come on, princess, come on a little bit. Or I'll sing silly songs 'til you can't stand it!"

Niki sang her made-up song in calm and quiet tones, keeping the words low and steady. Her dad had once told her that it was the tones that calmed a horse, not the words that were being said. As she sang, Warrior's head came up. Her ears came up, and she stopped prancing, too. She stared at Niki a moment, then lowered her head and ambled over, planting her nose right in Niki's palm.

Niki grasped the bridle firmly, pulling up a trailing rein, and Billy burst into laughter. "You are a nut." he said between the giggles. "A certified fruitcake! Where did you ever hear a song like that? Boy, you ought to sing that one to us on the bus!"

Niki felt her face begin to burn. *Why did I bother to help him?* she asked herself. *He'll never change!* She whirled around, gritting her teeth in anger. "For your information, I made that song up," she said. "You can laugh all you want, but I am the one who caught your horse."

Billy stopped laughing, but Niki wasn't through with him yet. "She wouldn't come to you, and I don't blame her!"

Billy's shoulders had dropped and he looked astonished. "I—I—didn't mean to make you mad," he said. "I was just joking around."

"It wasn't funny." Niki sniffed. "I should just turn her loose again and let *you* catch her!"

A look of fear crossed over Billy's face. "Don't! Don't let her loose," he stammered. "I'll be nice to you, Niki. Just don't let her loose."

Niki tugged on Warrior's bridle, leading the pony through the trees to Billy. "Fine," she said. "Here's your pony. But you better keep your promise, or I might be the next one telling stories on the bus."

"I will," Billy said. He stubbed his toe against a stone nervously. "Uh, thanks, Niki," he said quietly.

"You're welcome, I guess," answered Niki.

"Hey! Do you want to walk Warrior home with me?"

Niki looked up at the graying skyline. "I'll go part way," she said. "Dad will be home from work soon, and he'll be wondering where I am, so I don't want to be gone too long."

As they ambled down the hillside, Billy clutched one side of Warrior's bridle and Niki held the other. The mare's long strides fairly carried them along.

"You really have a way with horses, Niki Crawford," Billy said, and Niki beamed.

eight

"I think I'll ride her the rest of the way." They had reached the bottom of the hill when Billy came to this decision. "Will you hold her for me while I get on?"

"Sure," Niki said. She looked at the princess mare and she felt a tiny bit of resentment rising up inside of her. She had caught the pony, and now *he* would ride her.

Billy pulled Warrior over to a rock in the meadow. While Niki held the bridle firmly, he slid onto the white mare's back. As he gathered the reins up in his hands, Niki let go of the bridle. Billy gave Warrior a kick.

It happened so fast. As soon as Billy kicked the mare she rose up, until for one split second she looked to Niki like the statues she had seen in the battlefields of soldiers on rearing steeds. But unlike the soldiers, Billy Baily went sailing. He landed rump down in a soft, moist patch of grass and dirt.

Instead of running off, the mare stepped purposely toward Niki. She stopped just in front of the girl, head down, and waited for Niki to grab her bridle.

The carnival-like ride he had just taken didn't do a thing for Billy's temper. He came up and off of his rump like a cornered wild animal, all claws and squaw. "I'll kill that mare!" he screamed. "I'll break her of that stinking habit, yet." His fists were curled into angry weapons and he swung them in the air crazily.

As she watched him, Niki felt herself shrinking. This Billy Baily was scary.

He kicked at the bushes, the briars, the weeds. He shouted and stomped and roared. Then, just as quickly, he quieted and a rush of tears came to his eyes.

Niki looked away. Stroking the mare, she pretended she didn't see Billy rubbing the wet streaks from his cheeks. When she next looked up, he was running his fingers through the blond spikes in his hair. "Why does she do that to me?" he asked. "I wish I knew."

Niki was silent a moment. Then she spoke. "Maybe it was because you kicked her," she offered.

Billy's eyes grew wide. "Well, how do you make a horse go if you don't kick it?" he asked.

Niki was surprised that he didn't sound angry anymore. "You just squeeze with your knees," she said. "Real gentle. She will know what that means."

Billy looked from Niki to Warrior, then back again. Niki could see the debate raging inside of him.

"She'll dump me," he said.

"You won't know if you don't try."

Billy looked doubtful, then he brightened. "You ride her," he said.

"Okay." Niki said. She had been hoping that he would ask, so before he could change his mind, she led the mare to the rock, gathered up the reins and slipped onto her back. Niki sat still a moment. Then she swallowed a sudden batch of nerves and squeezed the mare's sides gently.

She needn't have worried. The mare stepped forward with a long, swinging stride, carrying her across the field with ease. She turned the pony in a wide circle, riding her back to where Billy was standing. They walked along a few moments, Niki on the mare's back, Billy quiet beside them.

"Wow." Billy said.

"See?" Niki told him. "All you have to do is remember to be nice to her. No more kicks."

They had reached the back of Niki's farm and Blackberry had heard them coming. He trotted up and down the fence line, whinnying his pleasure to the world. The sun had completely sunk behind the hill and all that was left was a shadowy half-light. Niki slid off of Warrior's back and handed the reins to Billy. "I gotta get in now," she said. "Do you want a boost up to ride Warrior the rest of the way home?"

"No," Billy said. "I'll just walk her. But thanks."

"No problem," Niki said, and she turned to grin at Blackberry. She heard Billy and Warrior moving down the path toward Billy's farm.

Billy had almost disappeared into the darkness when she heard him call out. "Hey, Niki?"

"Yeah?"

"Want to go riding tomorrow?"

Niki hesitated a moment. After all, this was Billy Baily. Then she thought about how different *this* Billy was from the one who had to be the center of attention on the bus and at school, and she thought maybe it would be fun to try. "Okay!" she hollered. "Call me in the morning."

"I will." His voice floated eerily on the shadowy breeze.

Niki slipped through the hedgerow and greeted her pony. In the dusty evening light he looked like a phantom, a gray-black ghost pony, much like the one who had pranced in her dreams for years.

nine

"Does Billy Baily's father hit him?" Niki asked as she shoveled a fork full of eggs into her mouth and watched her dad's face. His brows came together in the middle of his forehead like they always did when he was in thought.

"I don't think so," he finally answered.

Niki stirred the eggs around on her plate, mixing

them with the hash brown potatoes. "Are you sure?"

"I guess I can't be positive. I know he's hard on the boy. But I think it's mostly yelling and intimidation."

"Intimidation?"

"Yes. That's when someone uses fear to get what they want from someone else."

"That makes sense," Niki said. "Billy tried using fear to get his pony to do what he wanted. But it didn't work. Warrior wasn't afraid of him." Niki put her hand over her mouth to cover the smile that erupted when she thought of how easily Billy had sailed through the air. Instead, Warrior had made Billy fearful.

Dad saw her smile and his eyebrows arched into a question, but Niki didn't tell him why she was grinning. "What made you think that his father might hit him?" Dad asked.

"It was something Laura said on the bus . . . and I guess it's because of the way Billy is."

Now it was Dad's turn to play with his eggs. He

looked at the plate as if his thoughts were collecting there, somewhere beneath the mushy yellow-brown eggs and potatoes that he was stirring. "Children learn what they live," he said. "Billy will be what the people around him teach him to be."

"Sometimes he is *so* mean." Niki spit out the words angrily and her dad's head came up in surprise. "I'm sorry, Dad. But you wouldn't even believe how hateful he can be. Then yesterday, he was different. He was almost nice, and I felt bad for him."

"Maybe he wants to be nice, but he isn't sure how," Dad offered, and Niki nodded.

"He asked me to come over to ride with him today."

"Will you go?"

"I told him I would." Niki shoved the last bite of egg in her mouth and chewed slowly. "I just hope he's nice today."

Dad put his hand across hers on the tabletop. "I wouldn't worry none," he said. "You're just what that boy needs. A positive influence. A friend."

As Niki scraped her plate, then rinsed it, she thought about what her dad had said. It sure seemed funny to think of herself as Billy Baily's friend.

Niki rode Blackberry out the front gate and around the fence the long way, until she was on the back trail to Billy's house. She rode through the thigh-high tickling grasses, savoring the feel of the warm day and of her own pony beneath her. Blackberry swayed as he walked, and the rhythmic *swoosh, swoosh* of his steps padding through the tall growth was hypnotic. By the time they reached Billy's house, Niki was so relaxed she just knew that nothing Billy could say or do would upset her.

Billy was waiting inside a round corral with a post and rail fence surrounding it. Some of the posts were leaning and some of the rails looked as if they had been derailed. It was the first time Niki had ever come down the driveway, and she was surprised at how everything looked. From the road the farmhouse had seemed nice, but up close the paint was peeling and the windows were sagging. A winter wood pile had lost its balance on the side of the porch, and an assortment of spilled logs were scattered along its length like sleeping dogs.

Billy was trying to slip a bridle over Warrior's head, but Warrior was fighting him every step of the way. Something about the way the ornery pony threw her head made Niki reach down to pat Blackberry's neck lovingly.

A screen door slammed as Billy's mom came out with a basket of wet laundry to hang on the clothesline. When the door slapped back against its hinges a second time, Warrior sidestepped and Billy looked up. He saw Niki and his arm came up in a wave.

Niki nudged Blackberry and rode into the open area, out of the trees.

"Hey, Niki! What took you so long?"

"Chill out, Billy," Niki teased. "It's a Saturday."

"Warrior's ready to go. How about Blackberry?"

"Blackberry was born ready." Niki smiled at the phrase she had heard her dad say so often. In this case, it was really true. As far as Niki was concerned, there wasn't a more willing pony than Blackberry. Niki slid off of her pony's back and tied him to the gate. He gazed at Warrior, his ears pricked. Then he snorted and let out a friendly nickering greeting, his body trembling. Niki laughed and slid through the rails to help Billy with Warrior.

Billy jerked down hard on Warrior's halter. The mare looked stunned, but she just threw her head higher, away from the force of Billy's weight. "I take it back," Billy confessed. "She isn't ready to go yet, and she may never be at the rate we're going."

"Doesn't like her bridle, huh?"

"No." Billy grabbed the reins and slapped them against the mare's neck angrily. The mare jumped. "She doesn't like the bridle, but she will before I'm through with her."

Niki sighed. It was going to be a long morning if she let Billy have his way. Should she intervene? she wondered. It was only a moment until she had decided. "Want me to try?" she asked.

"Be my guest." Billy snorted, tossing the bridle to Niki.

Niki approached Warrior quietly. Although the horse was tied to the fence and could not run away, Niki still wanted the white mare to trust her enough to slip her head into the bridle on her own. There would be no force.

The same silly song she had sung the day before came into her mind, and she sang it again, softly, rhythmically. The mare's head came down, but Niki did not attempt to bridle it. Instead, she scratched the nose lovingly, rubbed the swirl of hairs in the center of Warrior's forehead, then touched the velvety soft muzzle with a fingertip. Within moments the mare had relaxed. The tension had left her muscles and her eye had lost its wild look. Niki slipped a finger in a corner of the mare's mouth and gently lifted the bit up and over her teeth. Then she pulled the bridle over Warrior's ears as softly as if they were delicate butterfly wings, instead of furry pony ears.

"Wow, Niki. You gotta teach me that song."

Niki handed the reins to Billy and smiled. "It isn't the song, Billy," she said. "It's all in how you treat Warrior. Any creature is going to like you more if you love it and show it that you care. If you are mean to Warrior and she does what you want because she is afraid, instead of because she wants to, you have no trust. I want a horse that I can trust, Billy, so I make sure my horse knows he can trust me."

Billy rolled his eyes. "Geez, Niki. I didn't know I was gonna get a speech."

"I'm sorry," Niki said. "It's just that you aren't having much luck with Warrior, and I think I can help you out."

Billy looked surprised. He leaned against Warrior's side. "Okay, Niki," he said. "Finish your speech."

"My dad says using fear to get what you want is called intimidation." She stumbled over the word, but Billy didn't seem to notice. "It doesn't work. Try love instead."

The even breaths of Warrior and the squeaking

of Blackberry pulling up mouthfuls of grass from around the fencepost where he was tied were the only sounds in the corral. Billy's face paled suddenly and he looked over her shoulder. Then Niki became aware of something else—the feeling that she was being watched. She turned slowly.

Just behind her, leaning against a tree and chewing on a long stem of grass, was Billy Baily's father. Niki realized, with horror, that he had heard her whole speech. He squinted at the glare of sunlight, then grinned, the grass slipping from between his teeth and falling to the ground.

ten

iki waited for someone to speak.

"Uh, Dad. This is Niki," Billy said, his words short and choppy.

"So I gathered," Mr. Baily said. Pushing himself away from the tree, he moved toward the fence and Niki. "What you just told my boy," he said, "it made a lot of sense."

Niki let out the breath that she had been holding.

Billy's father was an older version of his son, from the sunburned face to the spiky, overgrown, blond crew cut. They even wore the same kind of work boots. "Never realized you could get an animal to do for you like you just did," he said, "but I'm one that says if it works, do it."

Billy half smiled at his dad, his posture beginning to relax as he did. His dad laid a hand on Billy's shoulder. "How about if we try that, son?" he asked. "How about if we try what your friend there said?"

Billy just grinned.

After they had ridden on the farm for about an hour, Niki headed home. Billy had not felt confident enough of Warrior to leave the big farm pasture, but he had treated the pony better and he hadn't been dumped. *Progress*, Niki thought. *At least it's progress.*

As she rode home in the mellow light of late afternoon, the same feeling came over Niki that she had felt on the ride to Billy's house. It was as if everything was right with the world. The birds were singing and flitting from branch to branch in nearby trees. The earth rose to meet her with woodsy, warm odors that were delightful to inhale. Leaves swayed on deliciously warm breezes, rustling like whispering women gossiping on a midday break. Soon, school would be out for summer vacation, and the world would be waiting for Niki and Blackberry to explore it.

Niki patted Blackberry, then leaned down to rest her face in his thick dark mane as they moved down the lane and toward the barn.

Niki unhooked the lead shank reins and rubbed Blackberry down with an old kitchen towel. She rubbed the cottony soft material over his neck and back, then down his legs, one by one. She picked his hooves and brushed his mane and told him stories about how boring life was before he had come to stay.

When she was through, Niki put away her grooming tools and turned her pony loose in the pasture. Leaning against the fence boards, she watched him move to the dustiest corner and lower himself to roll, coating the freshly groomed coat with dust.

He stood again, shaking like a dog just emerging from a pond. He looked at Niki quizzically, then broke into a trot, gliding around the pasture in even strides, picking his white stockinged legs high in the air. He cantered around the field one time, two times, three times. At last he came to a stop in front of Niki. The dust had blown from his coat and he was as shiny as Santa's boot on Christmas eve. The white blaze that raced down his face gave him a comical look and Niki loved it. In fact, she loved everything about him.

You are beautiful, Niki thought, *and I love you*. It came to her that while Blackberry was still a trifle thin, he had grown considerably in just over a week. And in less time than that, she had come to love him. *He* was *the right pony for me*, Niki realized with a jolt. She leaned down to rub his velvety muzzle. "I may not have a princess," she said, "but I sure got a prince. You are my perfect pony."

*For more charming ponies
and a collectible pony charm, don't miss:*

CHARMING PONIES

A Pony Promise

A pony needs a mother's love, too.

Turn the page for a sneak peek!

one

Tiffany Clark brushed her long red hair from her face in one short angry gesture. She stared at her older brother Tim, her blue eyes widening in shock at what he had just said.

Thirteen-year-old Tim's grin faded. He dropped the bat he was holding. "I'm sorry," he said. "I shouldn't have said that."

Tiffany let the baseball slip from her hands to the

tall grass of the lawn. "Is it true?" she asked. Her voice was no more than a whisper. "Am I really adopted?"

Tim didn't answer, but as the silence grew wider between them, Tiffany was suddenly sure that the answer was yes. *YES*. The truth rang loudly in her ears.

"I'm sorry, Tif," Tim whispered. He reached to touch her arm, but she jerked away.

"Then, you're right . . . you don't have to play with me . . . because I'm not really your sister." She mimicked his words even more harshly than he had first said them. Her nine-year-old body shook with the effort of holding back tears. Her hair fell forward again as she leaned down, wanting to hide her face.

"Tif," he said softly, and his voice cracked. This time his hand came down on her shoulder gently. "Please . . . I'm sorry. I was just so mad at you. I don't want to take you with me everywhere I go. Sometimes us guys like to play ball without a kid tagging along."

She pulled away from his hand, away from the voice and the words that stung like a whip. "Then go play with them," she said. "I'm sure Billy and Mark are waiting at the park. Don't worry. I won't come," she added stiffly.

Tiffany watched him turn to pick up the bat and the ball. He slung the bat over his shoulder and began to walk away. Then he stopped and faced her. "You won't tell Mom that I told you. Will you?" he asked.

Tiffany thought a moment, scuffing her sneaker along the concrete ridge in the sidewalk. Then she shook her head. She wouldn't know what to say to Mom anyway.

As Tiffany watched Tim head down the road toward Memorial Park the hurt settled, crushing down on her like a heavy weight. *She was ADOPTED.* It rang in her ears like a gong. She had never even suspected.

Why had she never noticed before? Tim had sandy-blonde hair and eyes just like Dad's. Mom's hair was light brown. Tiffany realized with a jolt that she was the only red haired one in the entire family. Even her aunts and uncles had fair hair.

Tiffany brushed away the tears that stung her eyes. *At least my eyes are blue*, she thought, *like the rest of the family*.

Tiffany could hear Mom humming to herself just inside the screen door. She was capping a bucket of strawberries to make jam. Soon she would look out the window and see Tiffany. She would know that Tiffany didn't go to the park with Tim.

Tiffany didn't want to face her mother yet. She just wanted to be left alone. She needed to sort out the feelings that were whirling inside so fast they were making her feel sick. Before Mom could see her she ducked through the bushes that divided their yard from the Whiley family's yard. She walked down the driveway and on down the street. She knew where she would go. She would go to the pony farm. She often crept along the honeysuckle lined fence to sneak a look at them.

As Tiffany walked, the early June heat warmed her face. She thought about the argument. Tim hadn't wanted to take her along to play ball with his friends. But Mom had told him to. Now that she thought about it, Tiffany realized that she hadn't even asked to go. Mom was always saying Tiffany needed to get out with other kids, and that Tim should be proud to have a little sister that wanted to be with him.

Tiffany thought of all the times she had wished for a friend of her own. Now, she wished for one even more. At school she sat with Melanie Colmer at lunch, but it wasn't the same as a real friend. It wasn't the kind of friendship that kept other girls on the phone giggling or lasted through the summer. If she had a real friend, Tiffany thought, she could call her now. She could confide her secret. Tiffany had never felt so alone before.

Sighing, she crossed the street and slipped through the hedgerow, walking alongside the vine-covered fence. Tiffany always felt lucky to live on

Chincoteague Island. Other kids dreamed of coming here to see Misty's family and the wild ponies. They came on their vacations. But Tiffany got to live here year round.

She reached the main pony field and pressed her face against the fence board. She clung to the wooden post, watching the ponies that grazed inside the pasture. Everything seemed so different now that she knew she wasn't really a Clark. *Who am* I? she thought, and the tears came.

Through the blur of tears she saw a pony come toward her. It was the same brown and white pinto who always came to the fence to greet her. The pony pushed her warm muzzle against Tiffany's face. Tiffany stood very still. Then, a big wet tongue slopped against her nose and down her jaw line.

It didn't matter to the pinto that Tiffany was adopted. Heck, Tiffany realized, the pony hadn't even known she was a Clark to begin with. Ponies didn't think about things like families and where they truly belonged. *And*, she thought, *they never keep secrets from each other*. Tiffany smiled at the mare, rubbing the dark brown spot right in the middle of the pony's broad white blaze.

Tiffany slipped through the fence rails and into the pasture. She had never done that before. But today was different. Today she needed the pony more than ever. She wrapped her arms around the mare's neck, feeling the warm caress of a muzzle on her shoulder. It tickled its way up her arm and whooshed a feathery breath across her neck. Tiffany inhaled, relaxing a little. The pony smelled so good. It stood still, allowing Tiffany to hold her face against its neck. Tiffany's hurt began to soften and she opened her eyes slowly, rubbing away the leftover tears.

Suddenly, the pony tensed. Her head flew up and she let out a shrill neigh, trembling from her neck, down her shoulders and into her sides.

Tiffany slid behind the mare's neck and peered out, her heart racing. Across the field a tall, thin man with gray hair was hurrying toward them with an angry look. Tiffany recognized Paul Merritt, the farm owner. He was shouting something but Tiffany couldn't understand what he was saying. She scrambled toward the fence, slipping through to the other side.

More trouble, she thought as she slid under the rough barked board. Why had she climbed through the fence? She had known it was wrong, and now, even though she couldn't understand the man's shouted words, Tiffany just knew she was in trouble.

Big trouble.

LOIS SZYMANSKI

is the author of many books for young readers. She lives in Westminster, Maryland, with her husband, two daughters, and three cats. She and her older daughter have four horses—one of them a Chincoteague pony named Sea Feather. When Lois isn't writing, she stays busy taking care of her family, talking to students in the classroom, and dreaming up new stories about horses.

YOU CAN VISIT LOIS ONLINE AT
www.angelfire.com/md/childauth/